Away from Wood Street

MABEL ESTHER ALLAN

Away from Wood Street

Illustrated by Shirley Hughes

A PIED PIPER BOOK
Methuen Children's Books · London

Also by Mabel Esther Allan
THE WAY OVER WINDLE
THE WOOD STREET SECRET
THE WOOD STREET GROUP
THE WOOD STREET RIVALS
THE WOOD STREET HELPERS
WOOD STREET AND MARY ELLEN

First published in Great Britain 1975
by Methuen Children's Books Ltd
11 New Fetter Lane, London EC4P 4EE
Reprinted 1979
Text copyright © 1975 by Mabel Esther Allan
Illustrations copyright © 1975
by Methuen Children's Books Ltd
Printed in Great Britain by
Butler & Tanner Ltd, Frome and London

ISBN 0 416 83460 4

Contents

1 The letter *page* 7
2 Mr O'Donnell comes home 23
3 The new life 39
4 Trouble 57
5 Mayo says the wrong thing 75
6 Without a job 89
7 Bridget follows 104
8 Bridget thinks quickly 120
9 Happy Christmas 132

1 · The letter

"I'm getting rather worried about your dad," Mrs O'Donnell said.

Her three children, Mayo, Bridget and Paddy, paused to stare at her. They had just dressed in warm, shabby coats and scarves, and were on the point of leaving to go and meet their friends. For it was Saturday morning, and, in winter, it was their usual plan to meet in Slater Street at ten o'clock.

"I know we haven't had a letter for quite a long time," said Bridget, frowning. She was a pretty girl of eleven, with dark hair and blue Irish eyes. Her face had grown much more thoughtful lately, and, in many ways, she seemed older than Mayo, who was twelve.

"Nearly a month," said her mother.

"And that's not like your dad at all. I'd ring up the shipping company, but I suppose we'd have heard if all wasn't well with the ship. Only I'm worried."

"Has the postman passed yet?" Paddy asked. He went to the window and stared down into Duke Street. It was a grey Liverpool street, running uphill to the Anglican Cathedral, and there was a lot of traffic.

"I don't know. I've seen him pass very late the last few mornings. There's a lot of sickness in the city. Colds, 'flu and all kinds of other things, I've heard. It's this awful weather. So early in November, too. You're not to play out, d'you hear me? You've all had the sniffles these past few days. That's why I made you come straight home from school."

"There's mumps, too," remarked Mayo. "We've hardly seen the gang all week, but we did meet Mary Ellen in Berry Street on Wednesday. She said heaps of the kids in their school have mumps."

"Well, mind you don't catch them,

8

then," said Mrs O'Donnell. She began to write out a shopping list. This always made her look more worried than usual, for money was short. The sooner Patrick came home the better, she thought. She hadn't set eyes on him since May. He was somewhere in the Far East, but had said in his last letter that he might be home for Christmas.

"We won't get mumps, Mum," Bridget promised. "And I expect Dad's all right. There'll be word from him soon."

She, Mayo and young Paddy clattered down the bare, steep stairs that led from their flat. Underneath was an antique shop. It was going to be fun to see their friends again ... the Wood Street Gang, the seven called themselves. Though, in a way, they had been eight for some time. Bronwen Jones, who lived some distance away up London Road, was often with them.

The O'Donnells didn't go to the same school as the rest of the gang, for they were Roman Catholics.

Their mother had been born and bred in

Liverpool, but their father had spent his boyhood in County Mayo, in Ireland. He was a remote figure in a way, for they saw him so rarely on his leaves from the ship.

The cold wind caught them as they turned into Slater Street. It was good to think that their beloved clubroom was only a short distance away. It was in the old gabled building where Ben and Cherry Stanton's parents were caretakers.

They ran the last few yards, and Bridget reached up on tiptoe to press the high bell. It was a surprise when Mr Stanton came down the stairs to open the door. He shook his head when he saw them.

"I'm sorry, kids. You can't see Ben and Cherry. They both have mumps. The doctor came yesterday afternoon."

This was dismal news. Their faces fell, and Mayo said, "Oh, heck! I'm sorry, Mr Stanton. Poor them! But we could use the clubroom?"

"You can, I suppose," said Mr Stanton. "But the others won't be here. Mary Ellen's down with it, too. I was in the pub last night and her mother said there wasn't much doubt. And she'd heard Julius wasn't too well."

"All of them!" Bridget gasped.

"Looks like it," Mr Stanton agreed. "Seems it started a few weeks ago in several schools, and this lot are the latest victims. Ben isn't so bad, but poor Cherry looks awful and feels worse."

There didn't seem much point in going to the clubroom upstairs without the others. Bridget said she'd write to Ben and Cherry, and the three O'Donnells walked back the way they had come.

"We'll fetch our library books and go and change them, shall we?" Bridget suggested. "Oh, isn't it awful? How long do mumps last?"

"Two or three weeks," said Mayo glumly.

They paused to look through the window of the antique shop, and their friend, Mr Barlow, waved to them from inside the shop. They were just going in to tell him the sad news when Mrs O'Donnell came down the stairs from the flat.

"So you're back?" she said. "Well, come on up. There's bad news. The postman came five minutes after you left, and there was an air-mail letter from Hong Kong."

Her face was so grave that they were scared.

"Is Dad dead?" asked Paddy.

Bridget gave him a sharp push and mumbled, "You shut up, our Paddy!" But her own face was pale.

"No," said their mother, leading the way upstairs. "But he's had an accident in a tropical storm. He's in hospital in Hong Kong... been there about three weeks now, but he wouldn't let the ship owners tell me. Not until there was definite news of his return. He's broken his leg, and several ribs. They're flying him back to Liverpool any day now."

This was startling news. They all stood in the shabby living room and stared at each

other. Mrs O'Donnell took up the blue air-
mail letter.

Bridget noticed, with a stab of fear, how
worn and tired her mother looked. She
didn't look as bad as her sister, Auntie Lil,

who was plagued by her three little kids.
Auntie Lil had even less money than the
O'Donnells. But her other sister, the

children's Auntie Betty, was so different. She had married quite well and lived over on the other side of the River Mersey, near Arrowe Park.

"But our Mum shouldn't look like this," thought Bridget. "Will there be even less money now?" She was old enough to know the price of food and clothes, and what a struggle it all was.

She caught Mayo's eye as their mother opened out the air-mail letter and scanned it. Mayo grimaced, then shrugged, lowering his long dark lashes. Mayo wasn't going to be much help. He'd been in an awkward mood lately.

"Can I go and play with my stones?" Paddy asked, just as Mrs O'Donnell started to speak.

Bridget gave her small brother another shove.

"Don't you care, you horrid boy? You just shut up and listen. And don't start to cry, either. You're eight, and not a baby." Bridget could be very fierce.

"Yes, you kids must all listen. There're going to be changes. It concerns the lot of you." Mrs O'Donnell began to read.

"'So now they say they'll fly me back to Speke Airport, and an ambulance will meet the plane and take me to the Liverpool Infirmary for a few days. Seems they aren't too happy about my leg. It wasn't set as quickly as it should have been. I may be there only a few days after you get this. Everything's a right mess, or would be, if there weren't some good people in the world. We carry ten or twelve passengers, as you know, and one of the chaps – a rich chap – comes from Liverpool and owns some property.'"

The children were restless, not understanding.

"What's this got to do with us?" Mayo demanded.

Mrs O'Donnell silenced him with a look, and went on reading. "'He says it's no joke owning small houses nowadays, with repair costs and all. He's been selling soon as tenants die or leave. But this Mr Jenkins

15

says I was brave. He left the ship in Hong Kong, and he comes in to see me. I got this lot saving a pal of mine from going overboard in the storm. 'Course I won't be able to get up all them steep stairs to the flat. But we can have a house. Little place up Kensington way. Pearl Street ... Liverpool 7.'"

The three children had cried out in chorus. It was a cry of dismay and protest.

"Mean we've got to leave here?" Mayo demanded. "But we can't, Mum!"

"All our friends!" Bridget wailed. "Yes, I know I told *you* not to cry, our Paddy. But, Mum, it would be awful!" A couple of tears sparkled on her lashes at the very thought.

"It's not so far," Mrs O'Donnell said quickly. "Up toward the skating rink, I think. Up London Road, then Prescot Street. In this trouble I s'pose we're lucky to get somewhere."

"It's miles," said Mayo. "Well, mile and a half or two miles. Much further than where Bronwen Jones lives."

"Well, there's no choice," his mother said sharply. "Your dad *can't* get up the stairs here. Though I don't know where the money's coming from for the move. I won't read you any more of the letter, but we're going to hear from the agents who rent the house. You lot ought to be thanking God that your dad wasn't killed, 'stead of moaning about going away from your friends. You've got to help. Now I'm off to the shops."

She took up her old handbag and shopping bag and went off down the stairs.

"Away from Wood Street!" Bridget whispered. Once, more than a year ago, they had lived in an old terraced house in Wood Street, and later the gang had played in the house when it was empty. That was how they got their name.

Bridget dearly loved that area of narrow cobblestoned streets, with the old Victorian warehouses. It was not a part where many people lived. They worked there by day and went home at night. But it had character, and it was near the city centre and not far from the docks and the river.

"I don't know why they can't leave Dad in Hong Kong till his leg's better," Mayo grumbled.

"That's wicked," Bridget murmured automatically. "Mum's right. We *ought* to thank God."

"Oh, don't start being holy!" her brother said crossly. "I'm going out." And he slammed the door and clattered noisily down the stairs.

"You play with your stones and shells, our Paddy," said Bridget.

She went into her own room and shut the door. It was a tiny place, hardly more than a cupboard. There was just room for the narrow bed and a chest of drawers. On the wall over the bed was her beloved picture: a little harbour scene. The small window looked down into the back yard, where Mr Barlow's old shed had a row of seagulls sitting on the roof.

Bridget leaned on the sill, gazing at the

18

grim, grey scene. Nothing but brick walls and uneven roof tops. But it was familiar:

the place she knew. Home. And all their friends were near. Mary Ellen at the pub in Berry Street. Julius and his family now in their new flat up the hill.

It was very cold in the room and Bridget shivered, even though she was still wearing her coat. She tried to picture her father. His last leave seemed a very long while ago. That was when they had their May Day procession and their father had put his foot down over collecting money. He had said his children mustn't beg.

He was a tough good-looking Irishman, and he could be kindly. But he had a temper, and he was often stern. He had a horror of children who went wrong ... got into trouble with the police. He had always been particularly stern with Mayo, and Mayo resented it.

"Mayo's like our dad," Bridget thought. "He doesn't like to be told. He's clever, but he could easily go wrong. He's got an awful temper sometimes. I wish he wouldn't fight."

There was a knock on the door. Bridget always liked people to knock. She guarded her privacy in the tiny box of a room.

It was Paddy. His face was tear-stained, and he was gnawing a crust with jam on it.

"Bridget, can I go roller skating?"

Bridget hesitated. Their mother had said they mustn't play out.

"Well, just on the pavement outside," she said. "And don't blame me if Mum's cross and you get a cold. The wind *is* bitter, and I think it's going to rain."

Paddy sniffed.

"Everyone's cross an' upset."

"Well, d'you wonder? I'm coming down now. I'm going to help Mr Barlow for an hour. I'll tell him all about it if there aren't too many customers."

They went down the steep stairs one behind the other. Paddy was jangling his skates.

"Then this afternoon," Bridget said, "I'm going to write letters to Ben and Cherry. *And* to Mary Ellen and Julius.

They *would* have mumps just when we need them!"

She left her small brother putting on his skates, and opened the door of the old antique shop. The bell tinkled, and Mr Barlow, sitting in a high-backed chair, looked up.

"There you are, girl!" he said. He was always grateful when Bridget helped him.

Mr Barlow was going to mind, too, that they were going away.

"But it isn't *so* far," Bridget comforted herself, as she picked her way through the jumble of objects. "We can come on Saturdays. And there'll be holidays. We aren't going away, really. Not to London, or anywhere like that. We'll still be in Liverpool."

2 · Mr O'Donnell comes home

At Mass the next morning, in the little church in Seel Street, Bridget gave earnest thanks for her father's safety. Then, her face buried in her old woollen gloves, she added an ardent plea: "Oh, please, please, don't let us have to go away from Wood Street and all our friends."

But on Monday morning there were two letters. One was from the shipping company, explaining all the circumstances, and adding that Mr Patrick O'Donnell would arrive in England on Thursday, November 9. His flight from Hong Kong would be to London Airport, but then he would be flown on to Speke.

"Everything seems to be fixed," said Mrs O'Donnell to the three children. The post had come early, so they had not left for school. "He'll arrive at Speke at 4.30 in the afternoon. They're sending a taxi to take me to Speke. Then I'll travel in the ambulance with your dad, and see him settled in the hospital. And, d'you know, the Chairman of the Line has sent a special message. He says your dad was very brave, and there'll be insurance and compensation."

"What's comp ... something?" asked Paddy.

"Money," said his mother. "I s'pose that's something."

The other letter was about the house. It was Number Two, Pearl Street. The house was empty and could be occupied as soon as Mrs O'Donnell wished. If she would call for the keys at the office in Bold Street she could go and view it. Rent had been paid up to the end of December.

"I wonder if that's Mr Jenkins?" Mrs O'Donnell murmured. "He *must* be a kind man. I'll get the keys this morning. And now you lot be off, or you'll be late."

"It'll be a long way to school from up there," Mayo remarked.

"Oh, you'll have to be moved," his mother said. She looked worried and harassed. "I'll see about it today or tomorrow."

Silent with dismay, the three went down the stairs. The bleak east wind met them at the lower door.

"A new school as well!" groaned Mayo.

Clearly Bridget's prayer wasn't going to be answered. They would have to go and live in Pearl Street.

Mrs O'Donnell went to see the house that afternoon. When the children came home from school she told them it was quite nice. Two up and two down, and a tiny kitchen.

"There's a little bathroom, too," she explained. "Built out into the backyard. 'Course those houses never had bathrooms until recently. But they've had Government grants for improvements. It's all newly painted. But it's very small. Five of us ... we'll be falling over each other."

One of Bridget's secret worries had to be spoken.

"Mum! What about my room? If there're only two bedrooms where will we all sleep?"

Mrs O'Donnell looked at her daughter. She knew how much store Bridget set on that tiny room to herself. Not that she really sympathised with such ideas of privacy. When she was a girl she slept with Lil and Betty until she was twenty and left home to get married.

"The boys can have the back room," she said. "And you can have the front bedroom for now, Bridget. Your dad will need to sleep downstairs, so we'll put the big bed there. Later I don't know. We'll worry about that when the time comes."

Everyone felt unsettled during the next few days. Bridget never played her beloved pipe once. Bridget was a born musician and could get endless tunes out of her pipe. But she had to be happy to play.

Yet there was a certain excitement in

having a father who had been injured in a tropical storm, and who was being flown home from Hong Kong. No one else at school had things like that happening in their families.

When they came home from school on Thursday afternoon the key was under the mat. Their mother didn't arrive until six o'clock. Bridget had the tea ready.

"Well, he's come," Mrs O'Donnell said. "It all went without a hitch. The plane was on time, and I waited at the hospital until he was settled." She sat down tiredly and accepted a cup of tea.

"How is he, Mum?" asked Bridget.

"Well, he doesn't look so bad. But I never saw your dad nearly helpless before. The leg's in plaster, but he still has trouble with the broken ribs. Not easy to use crutches."

"Are we going to see him?" Mayo demanded. Paddy said nothing, merely stared over a huge piece of bread and jam. Bridget had made them wait, and now he only cared about food.

"He wants to see you. But as a rule the hospital isn't keen on children visiting. Likely they'll make an exception. His own kids he hasn't seen for six months!"

On Friday morning Sister Mary, the headmistress, said to Bridget in her soft Irish voice, "Ah, now, Bridget O'Donnell, and did your dad arrive safely?"

"Oh, yes, Sister." Bridget looked up into the nun's kind face.

"And it's delighted you must all be to think that he'll soon be home with you again."

Bridget blushed and nodded. "Delight" was hardly the word to describe her vague doubts and fears. Paddy had been difficult and fretful all week, and Mayo plain bad-tempered.

"Sister," she said, in a sudden burst, "we do love him, honest. But we ... we've never seen him for more than two or three weeks. He ... he's a stern kind of man, and he has *opinions*. Things he's always saying. The world is going to the dogs ... kids need

28

a firm hand. And he puts Mayo's back up. And, you see, it means leaving all our friends, and school, and everything. We'll have to start living different sort of lives."

Sister Mary nodded.

"You three and your mother. And now a sailor home from the sea, and with nothing to occupy him. But he'll be a grand fine man, I've no doubt, and young Mayo can do with a firm hand."

"But not too firm," said poor Bridget. "Mayo's a ... a rebel. He's all right when we're with our friends and doing interesting things. But, away from them, he'll get bored, and then anything might happen."

Sister Mary gave Bridget a gentle push, as the bell sounded for the resumption of lessons after break.

"Ah, it'll be all right. Don't you be worrying, Bridget dear."

It was easy to say that. Bridget wondered with unusual sourness if nuns had problems. Well, yes, they must have. Sister

Mary was head of a big school, with several hundred boys and girls.

Oh, if *only* they hadn't lived in a flat up a flight of steep stairs their father could have come home, and nothing would have been quite so bad. And if *only* Ben and Cherry, Mary Ellen and Julius hadn't caught mumps there would have been some comfort in talking to them.

Early on Saturday afternoon Mrs O'Donnell took them to the Liverpool Infirmary to see their father. The Liverpool Infirmary was on the way to Pearl Street, so she said they would go on there and see the house.

They walked to the hospital, along Lime Street, and taking the short cut through Lime Street Station. Mrs O'Donnell carried a plastic bag with some fruit and a cake in it, and Bridget carried a bunch of bronze chrysanthemums. They had been given to her by Mrs Murphy, the old flower woman at Central Station whom she had often helped.

After Lime Street Station the way was uphill, and Paddy trailed behind them, grumbling.

"I want to go on the bus," he whined.

"Not worth getting the bus with all these one-way streets," said his mother. "We're nearly there now."

There was a street market in Pembroke Place and Mrs O'Donnell found it hard to resist. Money was short for the moment, but there'd have to be new curtains for the front of the house in Pearl Street. She had her pride, and put up those old torn ones she would not. Still, that'd have to wait. She went firmly on up the hill.

"Now smile, the lot of you," she said, as they entered the hospital. "Look cheerful to see your dad on his bed of suffering."

In fact, Mr O'Donnell wasn't exactly on a bed of suffering. He was sitting in a comfortable chair at the end of the ward, watching television. He was wearing pyjamas and a shabby blue dressing gown that matched his eyes.

"Is that our dad?" Mayo whispered to

Bridget, as they approached. "Funny! I thought he was bigger than that."

Actually Mr O'Donnell had always been a small man, but he was so wiry and tough that you didn't usually notice it. What he lacked in stature he made up for, amply, in character.

It was a happy reunion. Mr O'Donnell's very blue eyes looked almost tearful for a moment as he gazed at his three children. Bridget presented her flowers as she kissed him, and a pretty young nurse whisked them away to put in a vase.

Paddy was shy, and Mayo rather gruff, but Bridget and her mother talked a lot for ten minutes, then they all watched the football match.

It was a much more cheerful party that walked on, uphill, toward Pearl Street.

But it did seem a long way, and every step took them further from their friends and the scenes they knew and loved. It was rather a dreary part, with no trees anywhere, and a good many big open spaces where old buildings had been pulled down.

"If we were going to have money for bus fares, it wouldn't be so bad," Mayo whispered to Bridget, as they reached Pearl

33

Street at last. "Paddy'll never walk both ways very often."

"Then the others'll have to come to us," Bridget murmured back.

"And what'd we do, in winter, up here?"

Bridget didn't know. There were no big stores here . . . no Museum and Art Gallery. Even the river was far away. And when she looked at the tiny houses she was sure there would be no room for all the gang in Number Two. The houses were in two prim rows, with their front doors and windows on the pavement.

As their mother fumbled for the key, Mayo and Bridget noticed twitching curtains in several of the houses. A boy about Mayo's age was standing on the doorstep of Number Four. The boy stared and Mayo stared back. He was a slim, fair boy, very clean and tidy.

The front door opened directly into a small front room. The O'Donnells all crowded in, relieved to be away from the staring eyes. The house was cold and smelled of fresh paint. The front room had been painted a cheerful yellow, and the back room pale green. The kitchen was very tiny, and the bathroom opened out of it. It took up most of the space that had once been a backyard.

"But I could have plants in pots out there," said Mrs O'Donnell. "If there's going to be compensation there may be a bit of extra money. Geraniums, perhaps, and ivies."

They couldn't find the stairs at first, but when they opened a door there they were, steeply built between two walls. Paddy jibbed at climbing them, for there was no hand-rail. Bridget told him not to be a baby and pushed him up by the seat of his pants.

"An' you a sailor's son," she said scornfully. "You'd never do on ship's ladders. Would he, Mum?"

"Takes after me," said her mother. "I never had any head for heights. And we'll

35

all have to be careful on these stairs. Your dad'll have to stay downstairs for weeks to come."

At the top of the stairs there was a space so tiny that only one could stand in it at a time. The door of the back bedroom was to the left. The door to the front one was facing the top of the stairs.

Paddy, Mayo and Mrs O'Donnell went into the back bedroom, and Bridget went into the front one. It, too, was painted yellow, and the window looked out into the drab respectability of Pearl Street. Once, though Bridget didn't know, it had been a slum. Now it was several stages up, but still dreary, with paper in the gutters.

She shivered, as she went to the window. Then, suddenly, her heart lifted with surprise and pleasure. If she craned her neck slightly she could see a vast view, beyond the end of the little street. Across a busy road, and a huge open space, the high buildings of the main part of the city rose in the winter sunlight. And, smack in the middle of the view, was the modern shape of the Roman Catholic Cathedral, with its lantern tower.

"Oh!" breathed Bridget. And then, "Mayo, come and see!"

Mayo ran to her side. He loved Liverpool and often took pleasure in its dramatic effects.

"It's not half bad," he said. "At least we can see it."

They had only been in the Roman Catholic Cathedral twice. They were more familiar with the red sandstone Anglican one that dominated the hill above Duke Street: at least with the outside of it. They had spent many happy hours in the great ravine behind the building.

The modern concrete of the Roman Catholic Cathedral was repellent to some people. But Bridget remembered the way the lowering sun had struck the multi-coloured glass of the lantern and spilled in rainbow splashes on the vast floor.

Mrs O'Donnell came up behind them.

"Our new home," she said. "This'll be your room for the time being, Bridget."

"When will we move, Mum?" Mayo asked.

"Soon," she said. "Auntie Lil knows someone who'll move us cheaply. And we only had to give two weeks' notice at the flat. Soon as we're settled your dad can come home."

They went cautiously down the very steep stairs, Paddy coming last. Then they went rather silently to the bus stop, as the last light began to turn thin and blue.

They had walked enough, Mrs O'Donnell thought. Bus fares were expensive, but what they needed now was their tea. Sausages and chips, and the cream buns she had bought as a special treat.

3 · The new life

They moved away from Duke Street before the other members of the gang were free from infection. But Bridget, who was a good letter writer, kept them all informed of what was happening.

They did see Bronwen Jones. She came down one afternoon after school. She brought Peking, her young Siamese cat, with her. As it was raining, he was wrapped in an old shawl.

"I heard about the mumps, and about you moving," she said. "Is it going to muck up the gang, you going up to Pearl Street?" Her little Chinese face was serious. Bronwen loved the Wood Street gang.

"How'd you hear?" Mayo asked. Mrs

O'Donnell poured her a cup of tea and offered bread and jam.

"Dad went to the pub. Mary Ellen's mother told him."

"We'll be able to come on Saturdays," Bridget said quickly. "Won't we, Mum? Sundays, too."

"Of course," agreed Mrs O'Donnell. The kids' whole lives had been tied up with that gang of theirs.

"And you'll be halfway to me," Bronwen said eagerly.

There wasn't much time for anything but packing up all their things. It was very dismal to see the flat gradually looking less like home. Bridget said she felt as if they were going to the other side of the world.

"But you're not!" Mrs O'Donnell said sharply.

The day they moved up town was grey and cold, with flurries of sleet. It wasn't a proper removal van that Auntie Lil had found. It was just a kind of small truck, and,

40

though they hadn't really much furniture, there had to be two journeys.

The arrival of the O'Donnells and their possessions caused much interest in Pearl Street. Curtains twitched on both sides of the street, and the woman from Number Four came to offer cups of tea. She said her name was Mrs Perry, and her husband worked on the railways.

"Three nice kids, you have," she said. "Irish? I thought so. I said to my Bill when you brought them up that Saturday, 'That lot's Irish. You can tell by their eyes an' cheekbones.'"

"Their dad's Irish," said Mrs O'Donnell, thankfully drinking tea. "But he came to Liverpool when he was seventeen. He doesn't even speak like an Irishman ... not unless he loses his temper. Then you could cut his brogue with a knife. I'm a Liverpudlian myself. Born in Knotty Ash."

"An' where's their dad now?" Mrs Perry asked. Her eyes were full of curiosity.

"In the Liverpool Infirmary. Had an accident at sea."

"A sailor? You won't have seen much of him, then?"

"Away ten months of the year," said Mrs O'Donnell. She put down her cup to direct the men where to set up the big bed. Then she went on, "But now he'll be home. For a time, anyway. You've got kids? I've seen a boy."

"Len," said Mrs Perry. "He's twelve. An' a girl, ten, Esmeralda." Unaccountably, she looked sad.

Mayo, Bridget and Paddy, who had been drinking their tea in a corner, looked interested.

"Heck! Do you call her all that?" Mayo cried.

"Ralda, mostly. It's a name I saw in the paper before she was born. Doesn't suit her," said Mrs Perry.

She went away then, since there was clearly no time for gossiping. The men kept on coming in and out, placing furniture.

They had a terrible job getting things up the stairs. At one point they thought they'd have to take out a window and haul up a wardrobe from outside. But at last everything was more or less in place, and Bridget had helped her mother to hang the new curtains at the front windows. Bridget never minded standing on a step-ladder.

They were pretty yellow curtains, and the last one had only been finished the night before. The material had been a moving-in present from Auntie Betty.

"Now I'll get a meal," said Mrs O'Donnell. She looked very pale and tired.

It felt very strange to sit around the table in the small back room. Paddy was fretful and Mayo very quiet.

"Esmeralda," Bridget said, to give them something to think about. "Why doesn't it suit her, Mum, d'you think? It's a nice name."

"Goodness knows," said Mrs O'Donnell. She had not missed Mrs Perry's sadness and her change of tone when she spoke of her

43

daughter. "P'rhaps she's a plain kid, and her mother wanted a pretty girl."

"Don't all mothers want pretty daughters?" Bridget asked.

Mrs O'Donnell flashed her own lovely daughter a smile. She was very tired, and the house didn't yet feel like home. But *she* certainly had been lucky.

"I s'pose they do," she agreed.

They all went to bed early. Bridget undressed in the cold front bedroom, then she turned off the light and peeped through the curtains. Craning her neck, she could see the centre of Liverpool spangled with lights, and a touch of floodlighting here and there. The wide, distant view comforted her, and she reached for her pipe.

Scrambling into bed, she sat up against the pillows and piped several tunes. The silvery notes sounded clearly in the quiet house. Mrs O'Donnell, just getting ready for bed in the room below, thought, "I'm glad she's playing again. I missed that pipe; Bridgie does play it well."

44

Bridget stopped playing when she heard voices on the other side of the party wall. The wall must be thin, so perhaps the Perrys could hear her music.

She huddled down under the bedclothes, shivering. They were at Number Two, Pearl Street, and Monday would mean a new school. Tomorrow, Sunday, they would have to go to a new church. Bridget had dearly loved the little church in Seel Street she had attended all her life.

"But we'll have to make the best of it," she thought sleepily.

The church was bigger than the one in Seel Street, and rather ugly. But Mass, of course, was the same. When they came back to Pearl Street, Len Perry was out on the pavement, playing with a ball.

Mrs O'Donnell went in to see about the dinner, but the three children lingered.

"Hello!" said Mayo. "You're Len, aren't you?"

45

"Yes." Len eyed them curiously. "Catholics, are you? Been to church?" He sounded rather scornful, and Mayo bristled.

"Yes, we are. And yes, we have. Any objection?"

Bridget tugged his sleeve anxiously.

"Mayo, don't argue. Don't fight."

Len laughed. "If it comes to a fight I'll beat you. *I* don't mind your being Catholics, though some would."

Mayo and Bridget knew that this was true. In certain parts of Liverpool there was a lot of prejudice. Their mother had told them that, in the old days, there had sometimes been street fights and real trouble between Irish Catholics and Protestants.

"Our mum wasn't a Roman Catholic," said Bridget. "She became one when she married our dad."

From the corner, turning into Pearl Street from the main road, came a girl. She wore a pink coat, longer at one side than the other, and walked slowly and awkwardly.

46

"Here's our Ralda," said Len.

Paddy cried, "Bridget, what's the matter with her?" and Bridget gave him a sharper push than usual.

"You shurrup, our Paddy!" she hissed urgently.

Ralda Perry was badly deformed. She was very small for ten years old, and her back curved, so that one shoulder stood up higher than the other. Her small head was thrust slightly forward. It was a sunny morning, though very cold, and the bright light fell on her face. She had fair hair under a pink knitted cap, and big brown eyes in a pale little face.

Bridget was warm-hearted and imaginative, and, after the first moments of shock, she noticed the unhappiness and sharpness of the small face. Ralda was certainly not plain. Her skin was clear, and her eyes were beautiful under a smooth, high forehead. But she looked unhappy ... anything but friendly.

"Perhaps," Bridget said to herself, "she's

never got used to it. She expects people to hate her. Or criticise her."

"These are the O'Donnells, Ralda," said Len. "Mayo, Bridget and Paddy, Mum said. We've just met."

"Hello!" said Ralda. But she didn't smile. She looked as if she would like to go straight into Number Four, but her brother was in the way.

"Hello!" Bridget said, and Mayo echoed her. Paddy merely stared. Later Bridget gave him a good telling-off for lack of manners.

And then Esmeralda asked, "Who made the music? I heard it last night. Like fairy piping."

"Fairies in Pearl Street!" Len jeered. But Bridget ignored him. Her pipe was in the deep pocket of her old coat. She nearly always carried it with her. She held it out.

"I did. I was piping in bed. Did it bother you?"

"Oh, no. I . . . I liked it. I never heard

anything like it before. How do you do it?"

Bridget put the pipe to her lips. An Irish dance tune pealed out, full of lilt and swing. Mayo protested vigorously, "You'll get locked up, our Bridget. Playing in the street without a licence."

Curtains twitched and Mrs Perry appeared on the doorstep.

"Kids, come an' have your milk. Ee, it's you playing that thing! Thought it was a street musician!"

"It is," said Len, and shouted with laughter. But once more Bridget ignored him. She did not much like Len Perry.

"I could teach you, if you like," she said quickly to Ralda. "If you like music it's quite easy. I've never had a lesson."

Ralda mumbled something and went past her mother into the house. Len followed. Mrs Perry paused to say to Bridget, "You mean that? Our Ralda does like music. Always listening to it on the radio. All that clever stuff, not just pop. The poor kid needs something. She has a rotten time. Most kids laugh at her."

"I think that's disgusting of them!" Bridget said fiercely. "She can't help ... being that way. Does she go ... to a special school?"

"No, she don't," said Mrs Perry shortly. "Her brain's all right. She's clever, see. Even though she's missed so much school, being in the hospital. They've tried; done tests and things. But they say there's nothing much they can do for her. She's stuck with it and she hates it. Who wouldn't?"

Who wouldn't? Very soberly, Bridget entered Number Two, Pearl Street. She was conscious of her own straight, healthy body that never gave her a moment's worry. In meeting Esmeralda Perry she had momentarily forgotten her own troubles and doubts. But of course they came back.

Next week their father would come home. No, *this* week, in a few days. Soon the changes would really hit them. But if her piping had really pleased that girl with the

51

sad brown eyes then it had done some good.

"And she could learn to play," thought Bridget. "It helps to do something well."

The children had not seen their father again, but Mrs O'Donnell had managed to see her husband for a short time every day. The nurses had been very good in letting her go in whenever she could manage it. The nurses, in fact, were spoiling Patrick. He was sitting there like a king, expecting his slightest wish to be carried out.

Many of the nurses were Irish and they were delighted with their fellow country-man. But there were plenty of coloured nurses, too, and they seemed just as bad. Or just as good; whichever way you looked at it. All on the spoiling lark.

"And I bet it was the same in Hong Kong," Mrs O'Donnell thought. "He'll be ruined. Expect us to dance attendance on him every minute of the day."

52

Though they had seen each other so infrequently, they had been married for fourteen years. Mrs O'Donnell felt she knew her Patrick. And she was well aware that he was not an easy man. His views were too definite, and his temper too erratic, for him to be a peaceful companion. Just now, in hospital, and pretty helpless, he was all Irish charm, but ...

It was going to be strange to have him home for longer than usual. Secretly she wondered often how they would get on, crammed into that tiny house in winter weather. Pat was all right when he had plenty to think about, and he'd always seemed to enjoy his leaves. But this was different. He was used to roving the world, and to looking forward to another journey.

"I wonder when he'll go back to sea?" she mused, as she lay in bed that second night in Pearl Street. "I'm sure the doctors aren't too happy about that leg. Though his ribs are mending fine, and he can use his crutches now."

She was sorry for her kids, having to change schools and move away from their friends. But maybe Mayo would make friends with that Len next door, and Bridget seemed keen on teaching Ralda to play her pipe.

"Anyway, when their gang are better I s'pose they'll all go down and play with them as usual," she thought. "Though it is a long way."

On Monday they all set off for their new school. It was a bigger school than the old one. Bridget bitterly missed her old teacher, and Mayo was in trouble the very first day for fighting in the playground. He gave a boy a black eye.

"But *why*?" asked Bridget, on the way home.

Mayo shrugged. "He said my eyelashes were like a girl's."

"So they are," said Bridget, giggling. "But why go and fight over it? Doesn't matter."

"I *felt* like fighting," snapped her

54

brother. He had no other way of explaining the restlessness that filled him. He had wild thoughts of running away to sea. Boys often did, in olden days.

"Don't you let our dad hear you've been in trouble," said Bridget. "He'll be home Wednesday."

Mayo scowled. He admired his father. He had seen all those far distant places and been in tropical storms, and was a hero. But also he was rather scared of him. Life had been so easy and pleasant with just their mother.

Mr O'Donnell *was* home on Wednesday. He was sitting by the fire in the back room when they all came home from school, with his crutches beside him. He had lost all his foreign suntan, and looked pale and drawn, though his eyes were as blue and noticing as ever.

"Well, you kids!" he said. "Here we are. It's not a bad house, is it? Seems small, though, after that big hospital."

The three children crowded around him.

The room seemed very full. Mrs O'Donnell said, "Take your things off, you kids. Tea's ready."

They obeyed and sat at the table. Mr O'Donnell heaved himself up with difficulty and took his place.

"Now," he said, "let's hear all you've been doing. Been good, I hope?"

They nodded, shy and uncertain. It was strange to be a complete family again.

4 · Trouble

Mr O'Donnell was glad to be home, but his ribs still hurt a little, and he hated to move with such difficulty. The cast on his leg was heavy and uncomfortable. He thought his kids looked fine. Paddy wasn't such a baby as he had been, but there was still room for improvement. Mayo was growing into a handsome boy, and Bridget was certainly a pretty girl.

Time he got to know his kids properly. Mayo needed a firm hand. He wasn't always as respectful as he should be. They had all been allowed to run wild. There'd be no more roving the streets. The city was a tough place and full of dangers and temptations. He had the golden opportunity to keep an eye on them.

Of course they were at school Thursday and Friday, and Mr O'Donnell watched television and talked to his wife. He also kept her pretty busy, asking her to fetch things or make endless cups of tea. He was secretly longing to get to the pub on the next corner. He'd heard, through Mr Perry, who'd dropped in, that the landlord was Irish. From County Donegal.

Several times that week, on the way home from school, Bridget had seen Ralda. Ralda always walked alone. From the back she looked very small and ungainly. It made Bridget sad to see her, yet she tried not to pity Ralda. She had a feeling that that was wrong. Ralda was a person, and probably proud. There'd be lots of things she couldn't do. Run, or play games, for instance. But her mother said she was clever, and so there must be things she *could* do well.

Thursday afternoon Bridget joined her and walked the rest of the way home with her. She agreed to go into Number Four that evening and give Ralda a lesson in playing the pipe.

When Bridget arrived the television was on full blast in the front room. Ralda took her upstairs to the small back bedroom. It was very cold, but private, and the sound of the television programme didn't intrude much. Ralda was shy and awkward at first, but she trusted Bridget's kind, warm manner and really wanted to learn to play. On Saturday her dad was going down town to a music shop to buy her a pipe of her own.

Bridget piped and explained, and Ralda was a quick pupil. Her pale cheeks grew pink, and by the end of an hour she had piped a little tune.

Bridget sat on the bed, wearing her coat. It was being a strange and rather upsetting week, but she was glad to help. In her secret heart she knew it was good to escape from Number Two, Pearl Street. She had left Mayo arguing with their dad about what to watch on television, and Paddy was in trouble because he had been noisy and whining. If she started to read her dad wanted her to fetch something or make another cup of tea.

In the old days in Duke Street they would have gone along to the clubroom through the little dark streets. They'd all have been making music, or reading, or playing games. The mumps would be over now. On Saturday they'd go down town. She longed to see the gang again. Meanwhile, Ralda was learning something new, and looking much happier.

It must be awful to have a twisted back. You had to live with it always. Bridget tried to think it out, while Ralda was piping, but it was such a big subject that it bewildered her. It was people's *minds* that mattered, really, and Ralda's was all right. But it must be a hard thing to bear.

"I can really do it!" Ralda cried, handing back the pipe. "It's like magic, making a tune come out. You know, Bridget, I've never had a friend."

Bridget felt guilty. *She* had plenty of

friends, but you could have others, and she had things in common with Ralda. Ralda loved reading and had a whole shelf of books.

"I don't see why not," she said.

"They all laugh at me. I . . . I hate nearly everyone."

"Then that's why you haven't any friends," Bridget said bluntly. "Kids can be awful, I know. But if *you* were friendly, and smiled sometimes, and let them see you can do some things well, they'd forget about your back."

Bridget dared to barge in, where others didn't feel they could mention Ralda's deformity. Except, perhaps, to laugh at it.

"But I *am* different. Even my mum's ashamed of me," Ralda muttered.

Bridget thought that might be true. It was terrible, but it might. She didn't care for Mrs Perry.

"Well, you've a friend now," she said briskly. "And you'll learn to play well. You can't help your back, any more than I can help having blue eyes. Or Mayo an awful temper. You could do well at a lot of things, then they wouldn't laugh at you." She paused, then asked, "Is Len clever?"

Ralda gave her a ghost of a smile.

"I don't think so. He's lazy, anyway, and he doesn't care. Listen, Bridget, you tell your brother not to get too friendly with our Len. I saw them talking outside after we'd all come in this afternoon."

"Why shouldn't he get friendly with him?" Bridget asked. But Ralda wouldn't say.

"It'd be better not. Honest. You tell him."

"I might as well talk to a brick wall," Bridget said. She was puzzled, because Len seemed all right, in a way. Always very clean, and much tidier than Mayo. "I'll come tomorrow. Give you another lesson."

Ralda saw her out and Bridget went back to Number Two. Paddy was in bed, and Mayo was sulking in a corner. His dad had won over television programmes all evening.

"Never mind," Bridget whispered, as they went upstairs to bed. "Saturday morning we'll go and find the gang. Paddy'll have to walk both ways."

They awoke on Saturday feeling keen anticipation. It seemed a lifetime since they had seen their friends.

"What you kids going to do today?" asked Mr O'Donnell, during breakfast.

"Go down town to see our friends," said Mayo.

It was an awful day. It was still almost dark at nine o'clock, and sleeting. But the clubroom would be warm.

Mr O'Donnell sat upright and stared at his children.

"That gang? The black boy and the kid from the pub in Berry Street? It's too far. I don't want you wandering all over the city in this weather. You said you wanted to join the library up here. You go and do it. Then play cards with me or something."

Bridget had flushed. Mayo was looking very angry, and Paddy's lips quivered.

"But, Dad!" Bridget protested. "They had mumps and we haven't seen them for ages. They're our friends."

"You can make new ones, can't you? I'll not have my kids walking miles, specially in winter weather. I want you all near home. There's too much traffic, and . . ."

"Now, Pat!" Mrs O'Donnell cried. "The kids miss their friends. You give 'em their bus fares and let them go."

"Right down there? They're too young to rove all over the city."

Suddenly Pearl Street seemed to the children as far away from Wood Street as if they were on the moon.

"We've *got* to go," said Mayo truculently. "So there!"

That did it.

"There's no got about it, me bold boyo," said his father. "You'll stay near here. How'd you get back in time for dinner? I'm not sure of me money yet. Not

64

wasting any on bus fares for three. You can go to the library, *when* you've helped your mother."

"We always help Mum," said Bridget.

"Yes, they do," said Mrs O'Donnell, much distressed.

"I'm glad to hear it."

Mr O'Donnell was starting to feel really sorry for himself. The first joy of being in his own home again was wearing off. His ribs still ached, and his leg itched under the plaster. He was used to confined quarters on board ship, but he hadn't been shut up in them. He liked an open-air life and plenty of company.

He looked at his children. They were sulkily obeying his orders. Bridget was clearing the breakfast table, helped by Mayo. Paddy, his lips jutting ominously, was making a bad job of tidying the room: moving newspapers from one place to another, and scraping up crumbs only to scatter them again.

Mayo was banging the cups and saucers

around so fiercely that he dropped a cup and broke it.

Bridget silently picked up the pieces and

mopped up the tea leaves. It wasn't often Bridget sulked. She was the best tempered of them all.

"No need to be clumsy!" Mr O'Donnell

grumbled, trying to move his cumbersome leg out of the way.

Mrs O'Donnell managed to get all three children into the tiny kitchen.

"Don't take any notice, you kids!" she murmured. "Make your beds and get off to the library. Then you might play cards or a paper game or something with your dad. He's bored. That's what's up with *him*. He hasn't even all those adoring nurses running after him."

"But the gang, Mum!" Bridget whispered urgently.

"You'll have to shut up about it for now. And it *is* an awful day."

"I don't know what we're going to do about it," Mayo said angrily, as the three walked through the sleety rain. Everywhere looked dreary and still unfamiliar. There was nothing *interesting*: just shabby little shops, streets of small houses and open spaces covered with mud.

"I wanna just go!" Paddy cried.

"Go? To meet the gang, you mean?" Bridget frowned.

"An' tell our dad when we get back. He can't hit us. We can just dodge."

It was unlike Paddy to make suggestions. Bridget was rather shocked by this one, even though she so much longed to go down and meet the gang.

"We can't, our Paddy," she said. "It'd be wrong of us. There'd be trouble, even if Dad can't move very quickly."

"Well, I think Pad's right," argued Mayo. "First sensible thing the kid ever said. Let's just go."

But Bridget wouldn't have that. She still had influence, even over her older brother. It would upset their mum and be unkind to their dad, when he was an invalid.

"It's only because it's such a horrid day," she ended her plea. "Dad won't keep it up. We *have* to see our friends."

They joined the new library and found books they liked. Bridget respected books and always looked after them well. She had taken plastic bags, so that they wouldn't get wet.

They bought a *Daily Mirror* their father had asked for, but he didn't seem to want to read. So they played Snap until it was time to lay the table for dinner. Paddy was good at Snap and often won. They cheered up a little.

But, after dinner, the day already seemed to have lasted forever. There'd be racing and football on television. That would keep Mr O'Donnell occupied for a few hours. Mrs O'Donnell said firmly that she was going down to see Lil, and she was taking the children with her.

As Auntie Lil lived in Seel Street, near where they used to live, the three children brightened. They ran for their outdoor clothes before any more could be said.

"Good on you, Mum!" said Mayo, as they set off.

"We'll walk down and take the bus back," said Mrs O'Donnell. "You'll see the other kids, but we can't be late back."

No, because their dad would want his tea. Everything now revolved around him. It was fair enough, but upsetting.

They all four went downhill as if on wings. Through Lime Street Station, along Lime Street and Berry Street. When they stopped at the pub to ask, they found that Mary Ellen had gone to the clubroom in Slater Street.

"She thought you kids'd be along this morning," said Mary Ellen's mother.

Oh, how dear and familiar were the narrow little streets with the shiny setts, as cobblestones were called in Liverpool. The warehouses were all closed, and everywhere was deserted, as it was Saturday afternoon. Mrs O'Donnell said she would pick them up at four and went on to pour out her troubles to her sister Lil. Bridget joyfully rang the high bell of the building in Slater Street.

And that time the rest of the gang were there, with Bronwen Jones. Mary Ellen's Siamese cat, Shang, and Bronwen's younger Peking were there, too.

The five children all shrieked with delight as the O'Donnells appeared. It was a wonderful reunion. Ben, Cherry and Mary Ellen looked pale after the mumps. Julius looked very peaky, and he said he'd been quite ill. Worse than any one, it seemed.

They asked endless questions, and Mayo and Bridget told their story.

"And we have to thank Mum for being here," Bridget added. "Our dad says we're not to rove the streets any more. An' he says it's too far for us to come down here. There isn't an *inch* of room in our new house."

"He means it?" They were all shocked.

"Seems to," Mayo said gloomily. "And I tell the lot of you, if this goes on I'm running away to sea."

"Our dad's just come from the sea," said Paddy. "We don't want another sailor, do we, our Bridget?"

Bridget laughed for the first time for days.

"Sister Mary said he was a sailor home from the sea. It sounds sort of familiar."

71

"It's a poem," said Cherry promptly. "'Home is the sailor, home from the sea, and the hunter home from the hill.'"

"So it is," Bridget agreed. "We learned it in school once. Robert Louis Stevenson. But that poem's called *Requiem*, and that means they were dead. Our dad's not dead."

"Easier if . . ." Mayo began.

Bridget really was shocked then.

"You don't mean it, so shut up, Mayo!" she said fiercely. "That's wicked! It's just that we aren't used to each other. Not in winter, shut up in a tiny house. An' he doesn't quite trust us. So we have to show him we're all right."

"How long will he be home?" Julius asked.

"We don't know," Bridget confessed. "He'll get the plaster off quite soon. But you can't go to sea unless you're strong. I think it'll be a long time."

All too soon Mrs O'Donnell rang the bell and Mayo, Bridget and Paddy had to go.

73

They walked over to the bus stop near the shopping precinct and waited in a queue of Saturday shoppers.

When they reached home Mr O'Donnell was tired of television and his own company. He said he was dying for a cup of tea. "But no one cares how *I* feel," he added glumly.

Mrs O'Donnell, determined to keep the peace, laughed. "Come on, Patrick lad! Tea'll only be ten minutes."

Bridget went up to her cold bedroom to change her shoes. Her slippers were so old that her right big toe stuck out.

The little house felt like a prison, and that was awful. She hated the family tension, and was uneasy about Mayo. He *would* run away to sea. Well, not quite that. Running away to sea was just something you said . . . a kind of wild dream.

"We did see the gang, though," she told herself. "And tonight I'll go and give Ralda another lesson."

5 · Mayo says the wrong thing

Mr O'Donnell was looking forward to having his plaster taken off. He was able to get around pretty well outdoors, but inside the little house, where there was not much space for moving, he was clumsy. He often knocked things over. When he dropped things he could not pick them up, and that made him crosser than ever.

"Frustrated, that's what I am," he said, often. He was always shouting for one of the children to come and find things, or rescue them off the floor. In the daytime, when they were in school, he still kept his wife busy.

But he *could* get to the pub on the corner, and he liked the Irish landlord. The Irish landlord liked him, and Mr O'Donnell really enjoyed himself for the first time for weeks. He had an interested audience whenever he talked about his days at sea. He could tell a really good story.

But mostly he only went to the pub when the children were in bed. And Mrs O'Donnell felt she'd better not persuade him to go earlier. She didn't want him to start drinking really hard.

There was still a lot of tension in Number Two, Pearl Street. Their dad wanted to know where the children were every minute of the time, and he was always watching out for them when they were due home from school.

"Don't you go lingering and playing out in this weather," he said constantly. The weather was a good deal to blame for the trouble; there was a lot of rain and sleet.

One day after school Mayo said to Bridget, "I'm not coming home right away."

"What you going to do?" Bridget asked, startled.

"Only play *football*," Mayo snapped, exasperated.

"Dad'll fuss. It gets dark so early."

"Let him fuss. You don't think I want to miss my tea, do you? We're going to kick a ball around for half an hour on the waste land over there."

Bridget and Paddy went home without him, and Mr O'Donnell did fuss. Mrs O'Donnell said, "Oh, let the lad play, Pat. He's too old to come running home like a baby. He'll come soon enough when he's hungry."

Mayo came home muddy, but more cheerful than usual. But his face clouded when his dad grumbled at him.

"I only want some *fun*, Dad," Mayo said crossly. "Anyway, Len Perry wants me to go to the Youth Club with him. It's in the old school in Ruby Street Wednesdays and Saturdays. Seven o'clock to nine. They play games and learn boxing. Can I go?"

"Sounds a good idea," Mrs O'Donnell said quickly.

Mr O'Donnell hesitated. Ruby Street wasn't far, and Len Perry looked a very respectable boy. He'd told his kids to make new friends nearer home.

"I s'pose so," he said. "If you come straight home afterwards. No messing around in the dark streets."

"Do they have girls?" Bridget asked. She longed for something new to do. She was restless, and there was nowhere to go but to Ralda's next door.

"It's just for boys," Mayo said hastily.

Bridget looked at him. Ralda had said it wouldn't be a good thing for Mayo to get too friendly with her brother, but she had never explained. Yet a Youth Club sounded safe enough.

So Mayo went out with Len. And Bridget went in next door to pipe with Ralda. Ralda now had her own pipe. She could play several tunes with a lilt and swing that impressed Bridget very much. They played an Irish dance tune together, sitting on the bed in the cold but private back bedroom.

Then Ralda played something Bridget didn't know.

"It's a bit out of a piano concerto by

Mozart," Ralda explained. "This is the piano bit, but you should have a whole orchestra as well."

Bridget was even more impressed.

Mozart! Her pupil *was* forging ahead. An idea stirred in Bridget's mind.

"D'you have a school concert or something at Christmas?" she asked.

Ralda nodded. "Yes. A concert first, then a little Nativity play to end the evening. I'm not in either."

"Why not?" Bridget demanded, and Ralda looked at her in rather a hurt way.

"You know I couldn't be, Bridgie. Stand out in front of all those people!"

Bridget ignored her tone and look.

"*I* think you should play your pipe to your teacher. You're ever so clever. You're going to be better than me. And I think your teacher will ask you to pipe at the concert."

Ralda was horrified by the very idea.

"I *couldn't*!" she cried. "People would stare at me. I always look awful, even in my best dress. Nothing hangs straight on me. You don't know what it's like."

"I understand all right," Bridget said firmly. "It's horrid for you. But your face is pretty. And anyway, people would be listening to your music. They'd forget you."

"I just couldn't," Ralda insisted, but her voice was suddenly wistful. Bridget left the matter there. She thought she had said enough. Ralda would think it over.

She said instead, "Mayo's gone to the Youth Club with your Len. Did you know?"

Ralda jumped and looked uneasy.

"Yes. Len said. Why'd you let your brother go?"

"*Me* let him?" Bridget laughed. "Mayo's older than I am. And *Dad* let him go. What's wrong with going to a Youth Club?"

But Ralda quite refused to say any more. They played two more tunes before Bridget left. When Ralda had shut the door of her own house Bridget stood on the pavement, looking up the street, in the direction of Ruby Street. It was a very cold night, but not raining. There were even a few stars. And, when she looked the other way, she

81

could glimpse the city glowing in the distance. Oh, were the gang just going home from the clubroom in Slater Street? Bridget missed them all fiercely.

Then she heard laughter, and Mayo and Len came running around the far corner. Bridget sighed with relief. It had been ten past nine on the Perrys' clock. It was silly to worry about Mayo.

She waited for the boys to reach her before she rang the bell at Number Two.

"Did you have a good time?" she asked.

"Oh, yes, we had a good time. Didn't we, Mayo?" and Len laughed loudly. Mayo didn't answer, and their own door opened then.

Bridget and Mayo went into the little living room at the back. Their dad was just turning off the television, ready to go to the pub. Paddy was in bed.

"Glad you're home in good time, me boy," Mr O'Donnell said to Mayo. "Did you enjoy yourself?" He was well aware that things hadn't been too happy lately, but he thought he had been right to keep his kids up in that neighbourhood. Keep a really firm eye on them.

Mayo was taking off his coat and didn't meet his eyes.

"Yes, Dad," he said.

In a way poor Paddy was the worst hit by all the changes. Bridget had Ralda, Mayo had Len, but he had no one to play with. Paddy, after a week or two of sulks and loneliness, managed to do something about it.

He announced at tea one day that he had a friend. A *new* friend, and she lived at Number Twenty, Pearl Street.

"She's in my class at school," he added. "An' I'm going to play with her."

"A girl friend!" Bridget laughed. "What's her name?"

"Delia Delaney," Paddy said proudly.

"Irish Catholics," said Mr O'Donnell. "I've met Sean Delaney in the pub. Now listen to me, young Paddy. You'll play near home."

"I'm eight, Dad." Paddy glared at his father. He, like his older brother and sister, resented being watched all the time.

Mr O'Donnell was sick and tired of his plaster, and not at all happy about his future prospects. In any other mood he would have laughed to find Paddy growing independent. Now he said, "You may be eight, but you'll do as I say, me bold boyo. It's nice you've found a friend. She can come and play here."

But there was no *room* to play in Number Two, Pearl Street. Paddy went off, grumbling to himself.

Mr O'Donnell went to the hospital to have his plaster cut off.

"Will Dad go back to sea now?" Paddy asked.

"Not for a long time," said his mother. She was worried, and seemed to spend all her time trying to keep the peace.

Mr O'Donnell was sent home in an ambulance. He was without the plaster, but he looked utterly gloomy. In a way he had expected the news, but it came hard, all the same. The sea had been his life. He had seen ports all over the world and always enjoyed the rough companionship. "I'm not forty and I'm finished!" he thought.

The children were just home from school, and were helping to get the tea, when the ambulance deposited their father at the door. He came in, still using the crutches, of course. He sat in his favourite chair and called for a cup of strong tea. Bridget brought it anxiously. Something was wrong. They all crowded round him.

"They say me leg'll be fine for ordinary living," Mr O'Donnell told them. "I'll hardly notice the very slight limp. Silly fools ... who wouldn't notice a limp? And all because the leg wasn't set in time. But the doctors say they don't think I'll ever get to sea again. You have to be a hundred per cent fit. Ah, it's the sad day for me! I might as well be in me grave, an' that's all about it."

Mrs O'Donnell had expected this news. She noted the typical Irish drama in her husband's tone and wondered what was best to say. It *was* bad news. She knew she ought to be glad that her Patrick would never go away again, but she couldn't imagine a sailor who never went back to sea.

"Oh, come now, Pat!" she said. "You're far from your grave yet. That's silly talk. You'll upset the kids."

Mayo and Bridget exchanged glances. Their dad home for always . . . no more blue air-mail letters from foreign ports. No more freedom. Bridget, soft-hearted, wanted to cry. It was awful for their dad. And it was more awful to wish that he would sometimes sail away.

"You'll have to find another job, Dad," said Mayo.

Mr O'Donnell was outraged. "Listen to the boyo! I just get me death sentence, an' he says I'll have to find a job. And what job could I do? Tell me that, me fine clever lad."

"Plenty," said Mayo. His dad could always make him feel small, but it was commonsense. His dad couldn't give up all idea of working.

"You shurrup, me boy!" Mr O'Donnell yelled. "I want me tea! Work! Me ... I'm an invalid. A poor cripple."

"Oh, rot!" said Mayo.

That did it. Mr O'Donnell reached for the nearest thing, and it happened to be the mustard pot. He raised his arm and aimed it at his elder son. Mayo ducked and the mustard pot hit the window. Everyone shrieked, but the window didn't actually break. Cracks spread in all directions, and the mustard pot fell to the floor.

Mr O'Donnell stared blankly at his handiwork. Temper.... He'd have to watch himself. Windows cost money and mustard was a nasty messy thing to throw around.

For a moment there was silence, then Paddy gave a nervous giggle. They looked at each other, scared and yet all inclined to laugh. Mr O'Donnell struggled with himself, then his expression changed.

He laughed ... they all laughed.

"Now see what you've done, Pat lad," said Mrs O'Donnell.

6 · Without a job

After that little episode tea was an un-expectedly cheerful meal. Mr O'Donnell felt ashamed of his show of temper, and his leg felt much more comfortable without the heavy plaster. It wasn't much of a leg yet, but at least it didn't feel the size of the room, getting in everyone's way.

"But I was right, wasn't I, Mum?" Mayo asked, when he, Bridget and their mother were in the tiny kitchen together. Mr O'Donnell had the television turned up very loudly.

Mrs O'Donnell thoughtfully washed a plate.

"Right, but daft to say it," she said. "Use your loaf, lad. Him just back from the hospital, and feeling sorry for himself. An' you barge in, like a fool."

"Not tactful," said Bridget. "But Dad will have to find a job, won't he, Mum?"

"Sooner or later," said Mrs O'Donnell, and hoped it would be sooner. But what her Patrick could do now he couldn't go back to sea was anyone's guess. "His leg won't be strong enough for a time. You just be good kids.... Well, you always are."

She didn't see Mayo's expression, but Bridget did. Mayo looked guilty. Why? As for being good, Bridget was getting tired of it herself. Some days she longed just to go down town and be free, the way she used to be. But last Saturday morning, when she wanted to go and help her old flower woman by Central Station, it had been the same old story. "I want my kids under my eyes. Not wandering away for hours."

When the argument came up again the next Saturday morning, Bridget tried to speak to her dad reasonably.

"Dad," she said, facing him squarely, "I'd be quite all right. We'd all be all right. Mayo and I looked after Paddy. We used to do

90

all kinds of things. Go to the Museum. That's lovely. They have an exhibition about old Liverpool. And, when it was fine, we walked up to Princes Park. And we ..."

Unfortunately it wasn't a nice day. During the week, when they were in school, the sun had shone coldly, but now it was drizzling and misty.

"But you were living down there then," Mr O'Donnell answered. "It's a long way from here. All that traffic. And it's a tough city. I don't want my kids ..."

"We *know* it's tough," said Bridget desperately. "It's our place. Dad. ... We want to see the gang. You ought to trust us to be sensible."

"Wait till spring," said Mr O'Donnell. "Different then, perhaps. Lighter and warmer. If the rain stops all you kids are going to take me for a walk this afternoon. I've got to use me leg. The doctors say I'm making quite remarkable progress. Those were their very words. You can show me the neighbourhood."

"Nothing to see," said Paddy, arriving at the end of the conversation. "An' *I'm* playing with Delia at Number Twenty."

"And not coming out with your dad?" Mr O'Donnell was a little amused by Paddy's jutting lip.

"No." Then Paddy added, "If you don't mind, Dad."

"Oh, go and see your girl friend," said Mr O'Donnell.

"Dad doesn't really need us," Bridget said to her mother, a few minutes later. "He'll stop and speak to everyone. Can't *you* have a word with him, Mum?"

"I've told him a dozen times that you'd be all right," said her mother.

"I wish," said Bridget, "that Auntie Betty would come over and speak to him. Dad takes notice of Auntie Betty. And she hasn't seen the house yet."

"Auntie Betty's been ill," her mother explained. "I had a letter yesterday. She can't come yet. An' why'd you think your dad would listen to her?"

"I think he might, that's all," said Bridget.

Bronwen Jones came up to Pearl Street occasionally. She brought news of the gang; it was a small gang now, without the O'Donnells. Mayo, Bridget and Paddy had only seen their friends once since that first visit to Slater street. Their mother had taken them down town one Sunday afternoon, when she went to see Auntie Lil.

Once they had gone down to the shopping precinct on Saturday afternoon with their mother. The precinct was very big, with several different levels, and escalators as well as staircases. The market was there, and Mrs O'Donnell could buy things cheaper than in the little shops up town.

It was lovely to be among the Saturday crowds, and the precinct was brilliantly lighted. Already Christmas decorations glowed on the big store across the street.

Mayo hated shopping, and was bored and

rebellious, but Bridget found it all very gay. A change from the dreary wastes around Pearl Street.

Bridget was still vaguely worried about Mayo. Every Wednesday and Saturday evening he went off to the Youth Club with Len Perry, and he always came home on time. But he was in a difficult secretive mood, and often quarrelled with their dad.

"Isn't Dad going to get a job?" Bridget ventured to ask her mother. Mr O'Donnell could walk better every day. He said it was because he had always kept his muscles in good working order. But he didn't go far. He spent more time in the pub, and was often in the betting shop, putting money on horses. It was no life for a one-time sailor. Mrs O'Donnell knew that, secretly, he was bored stiff.

"I dunno," she answered, frowning.

"Can't *we* find him a job?" Paddy asked.

"He'd kill us," said Bridget.

But she began to look at the Jobs

Vacant columns in the *Liverpool Echo*.
Her dad caught her at it, but he was in a

good mood. He had just won three pounds
on a horse.

"You trying to get me to work, Bridgie?"

he asked. "I've looked in there meself. But what can a poor old sailor do?"

Bridget looked at her father. He wasn't old ... he was a good-looking man, and he had charm when he cared to use it.

"There must be heaps of things, Dad," she said boldly. "One of the big stores wants a night watchman."

"Night work!" her father said disgustedly.

"It says 'Good money for the right, trustworthy man'," Bridget offered. And much to her astonishment her dad went down town to the store. He came back in a raging temper.

"Good money! Call that good money? And the hours. Upset me whole life working nights. No one to talk to. Not me."

"Mr Jones the greengrocer wants help," Paddy piped up. "There's a notice in the shop window."

"You'll have me sweeping the streets next!" Mr O'Donnell roared. "Use your loaf, Pad. Insulting me, that's what you're

97

doing." Paddy ducked from his whirling fist.

"They want hall porters and doormen in that new hotel on Lime Street," Mrs O'Donnell said. She had been looking in the *Echo*, too. It was now accepted that Mr O'Donnell would have to find a job, and they were only trying to help. "The Peters Hotel. It's a fine-looking place. Not far from the shopping precinct."

"Porter! Doorman!" grumbled her ungrateful husband.

"There'd be good tips, and you'd manage to charm all the rich people who stay there."

"Wouldn't waste me charm," Mr O'Donnell said sourly. He went off to the pub.

Altogether life was difficult, though Bridget and Paddy were quite enjoying school. Bridget's friendship with Ralda grew, and the musical sessions went on. Mrs O'Donnell was moderately friendly with Mrs Perry. It was best to get on with neighbours, but she didn't much like her.

"She gossips plenty about other people, and she's nosey," she complained. "But she's close about her own family. Never talks about Ralda. Or Len, except to say what a good boy he is."

Two days after making these remarks, she said to Bridget in private, "Bridgie, Mrs Delaney told me something today. And two other neighbours were there, and they agreed it was true. It worries me stiff, but I daren't mention it to your dad. Did you know Len Perry had been in trouble with the police?"

Bridget jumped and went very pink. Somehow the news was no surprise to her.

"No, Mum, I didn't know," she mumbled.

"You sure?" her mother asked suspiciously.

"Yes, honest, Mum. Only Ralda did say not to let Mayo get too friendly with him. She wouldn't say any more. What did Len do?"

"It was a year ago, seems. He and another

99

boy broke into a school and did a lot of damage. Just wanton mischief. And he looks such a good boy. Mrs Delaney did say he seems to have reformed. And that Youth Club *must* be all right."

Bridget was so upset she dropped a plate and it broke.

"If Dad knew he'd make another row," she said. "And Mayo'd be furious if he couldn't go to the Club."

"It's a problem," said her mother. "Mayo's awkward enough. You'd best not say anything to anyone."

Bridget wondered whether she ought to question Ralda, but next time she saw her friend she forgot all about it. The following afternoon Bridget walked home from school without her brothers. Mrs O'Donnell had met them and taken them to the dentist. So Bridget went by way of Ralda's school. As she approached she saw a most astonishing sight in the playground. And heard a lilting tune.

Ralda was standing there, piping. And girls of her own age were dancing. They all wore their coats and outdoor shoes, but they were dancing well. They were in a ring and, as Bridget watched, they ran forward, raising their arms and clapping on the beat.

Bridget watched until the end of the dance. She was deeply pleased, even excited. For Ralda was doing something well, and girls who had perhaps mocked her were enjoying themselves.

Ralda dropped her pipe into her pocket and came over to the gate. She was flushed and looked happy.

"Oh, Bridget!" she cried. "I played for two dances in school this afternoon, and Miss Blair said I was better than the record player. The girls wanted to do *Gathering Peascods* again."

"Anyone would like dancing to your piping," said Bridget. "Are you going to play at the concert?"

Ralda's eyes fell. "Miss Blair wants me to. I dunno."

"You're silly if you don't," said Bridget.

★

The next evening, Wednesday, Mayo went off as usual with Len. Mrs O'Donnell went to a meeting of the local Tenants' Association, and it was Parents' Night at Ralda's school. The parents went to meet the teachers and look at school work and art and so on. Ralda was helping with the coffee and cakes, so there was no musical session.

Bridget sat reading, while her dad watched television. But when Paddy had gone to bed at eight o'clock Mr O'Donnell said he was going to the pub.

"Keep the door locked, Bridget," he said.

At a quarter to nine Bridget longed for some fish and chips. Mayo and her mother would like some, too, when they came home. Quite often she was sent over to get them. So she lit the oven to keep the chips hot, took some money from the vase on the mantelpiece, and put on her coat.

She locked the door behind her and hurried through the cold, damp night. The chip shop was around the corner, just beyond the pub. It was steamy and hot, but not crowded. She was served at once and ran back.

Next to Number Two there was a narrow, dark entry. As Bridget pulled the key out of her pocket, she heard a strange sound coming from it. A muffled sound. Someone crying?

She moved slightly, so that she stood under a lamp, peering up the entry. In Liverpool one didn't go up dark entries. Bridget had too much sense for that. She just stood there in Pearl Street. The parcel of fish and chips lay warmly in her left hand.

Perhaps it was someone in trouble. Then she nearly jumped out of her skin when a figure rushed out of the entry.

"Bridget! Oh, Bridget!" It was Mayo.

The light from the street lamp showed that he looked unhappy and very dirty. And blood was streaming from a cut on his chin.

7 · Bridget follows

"What's up, Mayo?" Bridget demanded. She was shocked. "It isn't nine yet. What on earth were you doing in the entry? And why're you crying?"

"I'm *not* crying!" her brother said fiercely. "I was just gasping, because I ran. And my chin hurts. I was wondering how to face me dad."

"Dad's in the pub, and Mum's out," Bridget said quickly. "You come in at once, and don't wake our Paddy. What you been doing?"

"In a fight," said Mayo. He followed her indoors. Bridget put the fish and chips on a large plate and slid it into the oven. Then she returned to the living room.

"You look *awful*!" she cried. "All that

dirt on your coat, and your knees and your *chin*."

Mayo had recovered somewhat. The relief of finding his parents out had cheered him a good deal.

"Help me, quick!" he said. "Get a brush and clean me coat. I'll go and wash."

Bridget obeyed. Mayo dashed into the bathroom and she heard the taps running, vigorous sounds of washing. The coat brushed fairly well. Fortunately it was dry dirt. Bridget worked fast and hung it up, then squeezed herself into the tiny bathroom. Mayo's hands and knees were clean. His knees were grazed, but not badly. His chin was a mess; clean now, but still bleeding.

Bridget dabbed disinfectant on with a paper tissue and Mayo yelled with the pain. Bridget said, "Shut up, or you'll wake Paddy!" After a couple of minutes, when the bleeding was stopping, she found a large piece of plaster and placed it over the injured chin. She didn't speak again until this was done. Then she said, "Mum'll be here any minute. What happened? That wasn't

in a fight at the Youth Club. You wouldn't have had your coat on."

"I fought in the street," said Mayo.

"That's a lie." Bridget glared at him.

"You were scared. Why'd you be scared just over a fight? If you don't tell me the truth I'll tell on you. To our dad."

"Girls always fuss," said Mayo, but he knew she meant it. "I'll tell you if you swear you won't let on. Dad'd kill me. It was only meant to be a bit of fun."

"I promise," said Bridget. "What'd you *do*? Were you with Len? Did you *know* he was in trouble with the police last year? If you did, you're an idiot!"

"I knew," Mayo admitted. "But he's been all right since. I didn't mean to get into any trouble, nor did Len. We were just exploring. We thought it was an empty house. We got in through a window. An' it wasn't empty. There was an old chap living upstairs. He heard us and he had a great thick stick. I fell getting out of the window again. Then we ran. Len went one way and I went the other. I had an awful fright!"

"But ... haven't you been going to the Youth Club?"

"Sometimes. Other times we played in

the streets. Len has friends. It was fun. I'm
fed up with the way Dad's been treating me.
There's nothing to do up here. If we could
have seen our own friends it'd have been
different."

Bridget knew it would have been. She was
upset and worried, not knowing what it was
right to do.

"Well, I'm *glad* you had a fright," she
said. "Promise you'll never break into a
house again. That old man will go to the
police. Did he see you?"

"Not properly. It was dark. Oh, heck! I
won't do that again," Mayo said. "I'll never
speak to you again if you tell."

"I won't tell," Bridget promised, very
unhappily.

Their mother came home then, and Mayo
told her he had had a fall and banged his
chin. As he looked quite clean and cheerful
by then, she wasn't especially worried.

"They must be a rough lot at that Club,"
she said. She went to divide the fish and
chips, and Mayo ate his share with a good

appetite. Bridget tried to behave as usual, and her mother's thoughts were still on the interesting meeting she had just attended. Some of the local people were very angry with a landlord who wouldn't do any repairs.

Mayo and Bridget were in bed when their dad returned from the pub, and next morning Mayo just said again that he had had a fall. Mr O'Donnell didn't worry about that. His wife kept on telling him lads should be tough.

The only unhappy one was Bridget. She longed to tell her mother, but she had promised not to. Thursday and Friday she came fearfully home from school, expecting to see a policeman on the doorstep. But nothing at all happened.

Mayo just laughed at her fears. His lucky escape seemed to have made him bolder than ever.

"That old chap never saw us," he said. "And we did no harm."

"It was wrong to break into a house, even

if you thought it was empty," Bridget retorted.

"Oh, holy Bridget!" scoffed her brother. Bridget often irritated him. He was conscious all the time that he wasn't really a child any more. In his secret heart he didn't like Len Perry very much, but he had no other friends. And Len had a certain power over him. Mayo hated to be laughed at, and he was bent on showing that he wasn't a coward. And that he wasn't altogether under his dad's thumb.

On Saturday they awoke to find that it was snowing. For a few hours Pearl Street was transformed, and the distant view was hidden by softly falling flakes. But the snow turned to sleet, and by three o'clock it was raining.

In the early part of the day the three O'Donnells played in the street. They were with Len and Ralda, and Paddy and his new friend, Delia, made a huge snowman. The older ones had a glorious snowball fight. Even Ralda seemed to enjoy herself, though she could not move as quickly as the others.

But by three o'clock they were all indoors, and it was very boring. Sport on the television, and "Shut up, you kids!" Bridget went up into her cold bedroom to read. She wondered sometimes how long she would have that front room. Her dad could haul himself up the stairs now, though still with a little difficulty, because they were so steep. Sooner or later the big bed would be moved upstairs, and then she'd have to sleep downstairs. There'd be no more real privacy.

At a quarter to seven Mayo put on his outdoor shoes and his coat and said, "Well, off to the Club!" Bridget felt worried at once, but surely he'd really go?

As soon as Mayo had departed to ring the bell at Number Four she put on her own shoes and coat, and her woollen hood.

"Going to see Ralda, Mum," she said.

Bridget let a minute or two pass, then went outside. She expected, hoped, to see Len and Mayo going up the street in the direction of Ruby Street. But she was just in time to see them out on the main road, waiting to cross. Forgetting Ralda, she started in pursuit. All her fears were suddenly uppermost. They weren't going to the Club at all!

Bridget was very angry and upset. If she could have caught up with her brother then and there she would have hit him. Hadn't he learned a lesson, then? Was he such a reckless idiot that he was off with Len again on some silly, dangerous adventure?

But she didn't catch up with the boys. They were already across the wide road and heading for the traffic lights at a busy crossroads. Bridget dived after them, her feet slithering in the dirty snow.

It was bitterly cold. The kind of night to stay in the warm and not go running off into the windswept streets that were so unpleasant underfoot. She shivered and almost turned back.

Why should she worry? She was nearly a year younger than Mayo, and if he wanted to get into trouble let him! Maybe it'd teach him. If a policeman did appear at the door his dad would beat him within an inch of his life. It would be far worse than anything a Juvenile Court was likely to do or say.

But even while she was thinking this, Bridget kept on, with her head down against the wind. She had grown very sensible during the past year or two. She and her mother had been the ones to keep the family going, while their father was away at sea. It had made her older than her years. And real trouble *now*, while their dad was without a job, would be awful. Especially as it would so soon be Christmas.

The boys were heading down town. Bridget followed, a couple of hundred yards behind. The wide, very busy main road went downhill. Every bus that passed sent splashes of mud and dirty snow over her. It had stopped raining some time before, but it was horrible! And her old coat was so thin the wind went right through it.

She felt something soft and wet on her

wind-stung cheek, then glanced down at her brown coat. It was *snowing* again! Not very much yet, but it dismayed her. What were the two silly boys going to *do* on such a night?

She was nearer Len and Mayo as they reached Pembroke Place. London Road stretched ahead, brilliant with lights. But the boys didn't go that way. They turned to the left, then to the right, with Bridget scuttling unhappily a hundred yards behind. They were taking the quick way to the city centre, that passed the side of Lime Street Station.

This street was much darker, with very slippery cobblestones. The boys had never looked back, but, as they neared the side entrance to the station, they stopped and seemed to be arguing. Mayo half-turned, as if to come back, but Len took his arm and quite obviously drew him on. *Damn* Len Perry! thought Bridget, who never swore, even as mildly as that.

She was really scared now. She felt very

lonely in the snow that was whirling down faster every minute. There were few people around. It was all familiar enough, but she felt very young, cold and unhappy. She doubted her ability to influence Mayo even when she did catch up with the boys.

Len would laugh and jeer, and Mayo would listen to him. Or would he, if she threatened to tell their dad? But there was always the chance that they weren't going to do anything very awful. Maybe they were just going to wander around the big station. The old gang had once enjoyed a period of engine spotting. Bridget knew the station as well as anywhere.

The boys had turned in. She rushed after them, nearly falling. After the dark street, and the gloomy station approach, the station itself was brilliantly lighted and a hive of activity. It was only a quarter past seven by the big clock. Bridget somehow felt surprised it was so early. Saturday night in Lime Street Station was a lively time, with people and luggage everywhere. There was a loud announcement about a Birmingham train soon to depart.

Len and Mayo were not staying in the station. They left it at the far side and came out on Lime Street. Then they plunged into the subway that led to the other side of the street and to the shopping precinct.

Bridget followed, fifty yards behind. There were a few people in the subway and footsteps echoed. The boys were running now, up the unmoving escalator at the far end. The people who ran the shopping precinct must turn the escalators off when the shops closed.

Breathless, more unhappy than ever, Bridget saw the boys dart into one of the wide entrances to the shopping precinct. She reached the corner herself and peered after them. It was good to be out of the wind and snow.

The shopping precinct was very different from when they had last been there, when all the shops were open and hundreds of people were everywhere. Then the lights had been dazzling, the noise considerable.

Now the great place seemed almost deserted, and the lights were quite dim. A few shops had left their lights on, but many had not. The great passageway disappeared into the heart of the precinct, and the only people in sight were Len and Mayo, still hurrying along.

Then Bridget heard shouts in the distance ... shouts and loud, uncontrolled laughter. Far away still, a gang of boys appeared. Bridget instinctively plunged out of sight into a shop doorway.

She peered out cautiously. Len and Mayo had joined the gang. They looked smaller than the others, but Len was clearly being greeted. Mayo, too. But suddenly Mayo jerked around, glancing back, as if he would like to run the way he had come.

But he didn't do anything so sensible. He and the rest of the gang disappeared around the corner.

Bridget didn't *like* the shopping precinct

on this dark winter evening. She knew it fairly well, but it was a confusing place. She ran as quietly as possible along the wide

passageway between the closed shops and came to one of the inner halls. A motionless escalator led upward ... another went down. The place was on several different levels, and the city went downhill. So that if you went in at one end you were lower at the other.

There was nobody anywhere; only screams and loud laughter in the distance. Bridget walked up the unmoving escalator. She now felt in a kind of nightmare, but she couldn't leave Mayo.

It took real courage to go on, but she did.

8 · Bridget thinks quickly

"That must be an awful gang," Bridget said to herself. She didn't know how she would ever face them.

A man and woman went past her, walking quickly.

"This isn't the best place at night," the man was saying. "This way." And they turned down a side passage.

So even grown men were scared of gangs. But the precinct was a short cut to the Royal Court Theatre and the Playhouse. One or two other people went by, hurrying.

Then, as Bridget grew nearer to the laughter and shouts, there was a sudden, violent crash. A terrible, crunching crash . . . breaking glass. For a moment there was total silence, then a man's voice yelled,

"You young hooligans! I'll call the police. Here's a 'phone. I'll dial 999."

They might kill him before he could do so. Bridget stopped, terrified. But all she heard was the sound of running feet, going away from her. Then one set, quite soft, coming in her direction.

To her incredulous relief, it was her brother. Bridget knew what they must do and wasted no time. She seized Mayo's arm, ignoring his amazed whispers.

"Shut up!" she said fiercely. "*Walk* ... don't run."

"But that man's calling the police!" Mayo panted. "They'll be here in a minute. A cruising car ..."

"Just *walk*," Bridget ordered, gripping his arm. "If you run someone'll know. What happened?"

"Those idiots broke a shop window larking around. Meant to, I think." Mayo was white and shaking. If he had needed a lesson he had it now. "I'd started to leave, honest. I didn't like it. I was going away when it happened. But, Bridgie, how did you *get* here?"

"Wait till we get into Lime Street. The others went the other way, didn't they?"

"Yes. Oh, honest, I know I was a stupid fool. . ."

"You want your head examining," said his sister. She was walking steadily, shivering and shaking. Before they emerged from the precinct there was a loud sound of police sirens, but not near the entrance for which they were making. Bridget's whole being was given over to saving Mayo from trouble.

The precinct *was* a confusing place, even if you knew it quite well. Bridget didn't head for the subway that led to the other side of Lime Street. They crossed the pavement, and she, thinking the way was clear, began to drag Mayo across the wide street. The snow was falling steadily now, and the surface was dreadfully slippery. Agitated, scarcely knowing what she was doing, Bridget fell.

There were screams ... the grinding of brakes. Bridget lay in the roadway, within inches of the front wheels of a bus.

A crowd gathered in a moment. The bus driver, white-faced and upset, climbed out of his seat.

"She just fell right under the wheels!" he said loudly. "I need a witness. 'Twasn't my fault."

"Calm down, lad," said a big man. "I saw what happened. I'll be your witness. She just stepped right out into the street, dragging the boy after her. But the kid's all right. Just shaken, and very wet. And she's cut her hand."

Several people helped Bridget to her feet. The traffic was held up behind the stationary bus, and police sirens sounded near. A young, pleasant-faced policeman quickly took charge of the situation.

"I thought you were killed, Bridgie!" Mayo whispered. He had had two bad frights, and his lips were trembling.

Bridget, for a few moments, had thought

123

herself near death. Her hand hurt, and her coat and the legs of her old jeans were covered with mud.

The policeman took the name and address of the witness, and his companion, after a few words with the driver, waved the bus on. Mayo, Bridget and the policeman stood on the pavement, with the snow whirling around them.

"Where d'you live, kid?" the policeman asked. "And what's your name?"

"N-Number Two, Pearl Street." Bridget tried hard not to cry, but the tears were starting to fall. "Bridget O'Donnell."

"We'll run you home in the police car. This your brother?"

"Y-Yes." Bridget grasped at her scattered wits. Silly to have told him so much!

"What were you both doing down here on such a night? Really, parents ..." he muttered under his breath.

"Just ... just wanted to see the Christmas lights. We used to live down here, see, and we miss it. Our dad and mum don't know.

124

Please don't drive us home." Blood was oozing from Bridget's hand, and she was half-blinded by tears and falling snow.

"But..."

"Bring the kids into the hotel," a loud voice said. Bridget and Mayo jumped. A large man wearing a green and gold uniform was standing by them. Overhead, blurred by snow and tears, Bridget saw a brilliantly lighted sign. "Peters Hotel", it said.

"O.K., thanks," said the policeman. "Then we can see how badly the girl's hurt." He went and had a word with his colleague, and the doorman led the way into the hotel. The entrance hall was very grand. Like a palace, Bridget thought. She was grateful for the warmth.

There were other men in uniform, carrying luggage, and well-dressed people passing to and fro. Some of them looked at Bridget and said, "What happened? Is she badly hurt?"

Bridget and Mayo found themselves sitting on a green couch near the door. Luckily

125

it was covered with some kind of green plastic, so probably wouldn't spoil. Bridget sniffed and coughed and tried to wipe her eyes with a paper handkerchief out of her pocket. But the blood from her cut hand got over it.

A girl from a news stand across the hall brought a whole packet of tissues. The policeman said he would find cups of tea for them both, and disappeared. Bridget began to feel less dazed as the warmth seeped into her.

"Don't say a word about being in the precinct," she whispered to Mayo. "We'll tell Dad all about it later. We'll have to. But not to the police. They'll hear about that window later, and know there was a gang. You didn't do anything wrong, so . . ."

Mayo just nodded. He was still white-faced.

The policeman brought the tea. It was very sweet and piping hot. Bridget drank some and felt almost herself. She glanced around the wonderful new hotel, deeply impressed. She saw the doorman who had led them in carrying some very expensive-looking luggage. A man who had an American accent slipped him a whole pound.

Bridget heard the crackle of the note and the doorman's gratified, "Thank you, sir!"

The Peters Hotel! Porters and doormen wanted . . . in the *Liverpool Echo*. And their dad had said he wouldn't waste his charm. But this would be a wonderful place for him to work. Bridget jumped and spilled some tea when a voice asked, "What's going on, Officer? I heard there'd been an accident."

"Not much of a one," the young policeman said. "But the girl's hurt her hand, and she was very shaken up. Her colour's coming back. She'll be all right."

"I'm Blake, the assistant manager," the man explained. He was very beautifully dressed in a dark suit and a discreet tie. "Poor children! What's your name?" he asked Bridget.

"Bridget O'Donnell . . . sir," she said.

"Letting kids wander around far from home on a night like this!" the policeman muttered. "But they said their dad didn't know."

Bridget finished her tea and stood up. They'd have to get home, and she felt strong enough now. But not in a police car ... they'd have to drag her into one.

The assistant manager was still hovering. He looked kind and sympathetic.

"Mr Blake," Bridget said boldly. Oh, if only some good could come out of this dreadful evening! "Mr Blake, Mum saw in the *Echo* ... There was an advert about wanting doormen and porters."

Mr Blake looked astonished, then amused. Among all the prosperous people Bridget looked draggled and very small. But she suddenly had a kind of dignity. In spite of her wet hair straggling from under her old woollen hood, she was a very pretty girl.

"That's right," he agreed. "We still want another doorman. Two entrances to this hotel, and they have to be manned twenty-four hours a day, seven days a week." He looked at Mayo, who was staring at Bridget. "Wanting a job, son?" he asked jokingly.

Mayo, too, had recovered. He knew he still had a lot of explaining to do, but no one knew about the precinct.

"Our Bridget's thinking of Dad," he said. "You see, Dad's always been a sailor. Twenty years with the Golden Crown Line. An' he had an accident at sea, saving his mate in a storm. He broke his leg, and now it won't be good enough for the sea. But he'd make a grand doorman, our dad. He's handsome and ... and trustworthy."

"Irish," murmured the assistant manager. "Half our staff are Irish. But I'd have to see him, you know."

"If I'm not mistaken," said the young policeman, "here's the gentleman himself."

Bridget and Mayo gasped and turned. Through the swing door came first a policeman, followed by their dad. Behind their dad came – astonishingly – Auntie Betty. Auntie Betty wore a very smart dark red raincoat and shiny black boots.

Mr O'Donnell, blinking in the bright lights, spied the little group by the green couch. He looked angry and bewildered. He limped over to them and demanded,

"What's all this? What you two doing down here? When the police car came for me ..."

Bridget and Mayo were speechless, but Mr Blake was not.

"It's a bit public here," he said. "Let's go into my office."

The policemen said they'd wait outside, but not to be long. The snow was getting worse, and they'd all be better at home. The one who had been present all the time looked amused and interested.

"Your dad'll get that job," he whispered.

Bridget, Mayo, Auntie Betty and Mr O'Donnell crowded into the office. For a few minutes all was confusion, but gradually Mr O'Donnell calmed down. This was mostly due to Auntie Betty. She was always a calm person, in command of any situation. Bridget was deeply glad that she was there. She didn't yet know *how* she was there, but it was wonderful.

9 · Happy Christmas

It was Auntie Betty who said Bridget and Mayo could explain later why they were so naughty as to be down town. As long as Bridget wasn't badly hurt, it would all wait until they reached home.

Mr Blake chipped in, "Mr O'Donnell, your daughter says you want a job. And we need a doorman. It's quite a good job. Uniform provided, fair wages, and excellent tips. This is a good class hotel. Your son says you were twenty years with the Golden Crown Line, so no doubt they'd give you a reference."

Mr O'Donnell was still bewildered by all that had happened, but he had noticed the grandeur of the hotel. The splendour of the green and gold uniform. It'd mean working nights sometimes, but not like being a night watchman in some store. Here there'd be warmth and company. In some part of his mind he thought that the uniform would suit him fine.

"I got to have a job," he said. "But you'll be knowing it isn't easy for a sailor ..."

"You think about it," said Mr Blake. "And come down and see me in the morning. Sunday, I know, but I'll be here. If it works out we'd like you to start almost at once. Christmas is our busy time. If that leg still bothers you, you can have a stool. Needn't stand all the time."

"Oh, Dad!" Bridget breathed.

"Now you'd better not keep the police waiting," said Mr Blake. He patted Bridget's damp shoulder. "You be a good girl in future. And always watch the traffic."

They were put into the back of the police car. There was just room, if Bridget sat on Auntie Betty's knee. As they drove up town by roundabout ways, because of the one-way streets, Bridget said to Auntie Betty,

133

"Oh, I was so glad to see you! Mum said you'd been ill. But it's snowing hard. How'll you get home later?"

"I'm better now," Auntie Betty said cheerfully. "And I've come to spend the night. I brought my nightie and toothbrush with me. It was a sudden thought. I had a letter from your mother. So I'm going to share your bed, Bridget. I'd only been in Pearl Street twenty minutes when the policeman rang the bell. I said I'd come down to get you. Your poor mother stayed with Paddy. She'll be very worried."

"There's some explaining to do," Mr O'Donnell said.

The explaining wasn't very pleasant for Mayo. But he had had a really bad scare, and he told the whole truth. Mr O'Donnell was furious at first and threatened his son with a good beating. But Auntie Betty intervened.

"Now wait, Pat!" she said firmly. "The lad's been a fool, and your Bridget was brave to go after him and keep the whole thing from the police. Quick-witted, she is. Mayo hadn't had anything to do with that broken window, so it was right enough to keep him out of it. He won't go with that gang again."

"And sure he will not!" said Mr O'Donnell.

"But really you have two sensible kids. It was just ill luck that Bridget was upset and stepped into the traffic. She won't do that again. They've always struck me as being independent and able to use their heads. You've kept them too cooped up. Fancy not letting them go down to see their friends! You've been a bit of a fool, Pat, so . . ."

"Me a fool!" Mr O'Donnell shouted. "Most parents don't seem to care. I was trying to keep 'em under me own eyes."

"Well, of course you care. But Mayo's a big lad now, and sensible really. Paddy never came to any harm when he was with the others, either."

"Mind your own business, Betty!"

Auntie Betty laughed.

135

"I never could. And I know things haven't been very happy here. You take that job, Pat. You'll be down town, and perhaps the kids can go down with you, or meet you at the end of your shift to come home. Just in winter. In the lighter days they'll be fine. Trust them. Give 'em money for bus fares. You'll not be hard up."

Mr O'Donnell fought with himself. He hated to admit he had been wrong. He caught his wife's eye and smiled.

"I suppose you're right, Betty," he said reluctantly. "One thing I do see now. Those Wood Street kids are better than Len Perry. You'll have no more to do with Len, Mayo."

"He won't go out with Len, Pat," Mrs O'Donnell said quickly. "But we can't actually quarrel with the Perrys. There's Ralda to think of. Bridget's taken her on, and I've seen for myself she's a different girl. Much brighter."

They had to live with their Pearl Street neighbours. Mr O'Donnell saw that.

Bridget said to Auntie Betty, when they were in bed together, "Oh, it was luck that you came tonight! Everything was awful. But you do think we'll be all right now?"

"It will work out fine," said Auntie Betty. "Your dad will be a different man when he has a job. You needn't worry any more. You do a deal too much worrying for your age."

Everything did work out fine. Mr O'Donnell was given a good reference, and he was to start work at the Peters Hotel on Christmas Eve.

Bridget told Ralda the whole story, though she knew some of it already from Len. Len hadn't been picked up by the police, but he had had a bad fright. He hadn't had a hand in breaking the window, but he was going to be a more cautious boy for some time to come.

Ralda was excited and nervous. She was going to play her pipe at the school concert on the last night of term. Bridget went as a guest. She felt as nervous as Ralda, for she knew it was taking all her friend's courage to stand on the platform in front of the big audience.

Ralda stood there alone and piped tune after tune. Soon people were tapping their feet to the wonderful rhythm. They clapped and clapped and asked for more. Ralda, flushed and pretty, played again.

Ralda would always have her problems, but she took a big step forward that night.

"It was all due to you, Bridget," she said the next day.

Bridget brushed that aside.

"Ralda," she said, "sometimes you're coming down with us to be with the Wood Street gang. You're going to play in our pop group."

Christmas was lovely. Mr O'Donnell had to work some of the time, but he didn't seem to mind. He was busy establishing himself as a character at the Peters Hotel. And the Christmas tips were extra good. He would

138

always miss the sea, of course, but he was meeting plenty of people. That was what he enjoyed.

"Listen, you kids," he said, two days after

Christmas. The three children had been down town to have tea with the gang at

Julius's, and had met their dad to come home. "I've been thinking. When I get me holidays we'll go to Ireland. We'll take the night boat to Dublin. You'll like that, won't you? We'll go over to County Mayo and see me sister again."

Ireland! It was nearly two and a half years since they had been there, but Bridget had never forgotten. She thought of the great conical mountain, Croag Patrick, and the lovely little roads of County Mayo ... the beautiful sea that washed the rocky coast.

"Oh, Dad!" she cried. "That'll be best of all."